Attack of the Evil Elvises

For Judith and Zack. The truth is out there.
                                                    —*D.G.*

weirdplanet 4

Attack of the Evil Elvises

by Dan Greenburg

illustrated by Macky Pamintuan

A STEPPING STONE BOOK™

Random House 🏠 New York

Copyright © 2007 by Dan Greenburg
Illustrations copyright © 2007 by Macky Pamintuan

Published in the United States by Random House Children's Books,
a division of Random House, Inc., New York.

RANDOM HOUSE and colophon are registered trademarks and
A STEPPING STONE BOOK and colophon are trademarks of
Random House, Inc.

www.steppingstonesbooks.com
www.randomhouse.com/kids

Educators and librarians, for a variety of teaching tools, visit us at
www.randomhouse.com/teachers

Library of Congress Cataloging-in-Publication Data
Greenburg, Dan.
Attack of the evil Elvises / by Dan Greenburg ;
illustrated by Macky Pamintuan. — 1st ed.
p.   cm. — (Weird planet ; 4)
"A Stepping Stone Book."
SUMMARY: Siblings Klatu, Lek, and Ploo from the planet Loogl return to Las Vegas, where they discover an impending invasion of Earth by evil aliens disguised as Elvis impersonators.
ISBN: 978-0-375-83347-2 (pbk.)
ISBN: 978-0-375-93347-9 (lib. bdg.)
[1. Extraterrestrial beings—Fiction. 2. Brothers and sisters—Fiction. 3. Las Vegas (Nev.)—Fiction. 4. Science fiction. 5. Humorous stories.]
I. Pamintuan, Macky, ill. II. Title. III. Series: Greenburg, Dan. Weird planet ; 4.
PZ7.G8278At 2007
[Fic]—dc22   2006017483

Printed in the United States of America
10 9 8 7 6 5 4 3 2 1
First Edition

Contents

The Monster in the Trunk

Back and forth. Back and forth. Ploo felt like she'd been driven between Area 51 and Las Vegas about a million times already. She studied her face in the car's mirror.

Could there be a prettier skin color in the entire universe than my lovely shade of gray? she wondered. *Hardly. Could there be anything prettier growing out of anyone's head than my curly antenna? Never.*

Ploo was an alien from the planet Loogl. A few days ago, she and her two brothers had crash-landed their spaceship in the Nevada desert. Now they were all in their human friend Jo-Jo's pink Cadillac. And they were going back to Las Vegas. Again.

"I am not at all worried," said Klatu, Ploo's older brother. He looked outside at the desert. The sun had just set and the cactuses stood black against the pink and tan sky.

What are you not worried about? Ploo spoke directly to her brother's mind using E.S.P.

"About the Great Ones," said Klatu out loud. "They promised to send back a spaceship to pick us up. I believe them."

Why do you believe them? esped Ploo.

"They have never failed us yet," said Klatu.

"But, Klatu, they've never had a *chance* to fail you yet, darlin'," said Jo-Jo. "You just met them." Jo-Jo was a blond woman from Texas who sounded as though she had never left there.

"I am still not worried," said Klatu.

"Well, *I* am," said Lek. Lek was Klatu's brother. He was younger and smaller than Klatu but older and larger than Ploo. "Although the Great Ones are Looglings like us, and great, I do not trust them at all. I do not even like them."

"If and when they do contact y'all," said Jo-Jo, "I'll take you back to the desert to meet the spaceship. Till then, I'll try to keep y'all out of trouble."

Jo-Jo had been a mechanic at the Area 51 army base. She'd repaired crashed UFOs there for years. She quit when she got tired of taking orders.

"What if they never come for us?" Lek asked.

"Then I might have to build y'all a spaceship from scratch," said Jo-Jo.

Klatu was impressed. "If I have an itch and I scratch it, you could build a spaceship from this?" he said.

Suddenly they heard a mysterious knocking noise in the trunk.

"What is that knocking noise?" said Klatu.

Jo-Jo frowned. "I don't hardly know, hon. It doesn't sound mechanical," she said.

Lek was worried. "It might be a monster," he said.

The knocking noise came again. A series of dull thuds. It sounded as though some living thing was trapped inside. Lek shuddered. Jo-Jo stopped the car. "Let's go see what's makin' that noise," she said.

"Good," said Klatu. "I shall stay here and protect the car."

"And I shall stay here and protect Klatu," said Lek.

Jo-Jo and Ploo got out of the car to take a look. The desert was quiet except for the *creek*ing of crickets. Jo-Jo walked back to the trunk and opened it.

A small girl with curly blond hair poked her head out. It was Lily, the daughter of Major Paine. Major Paine was the commander of the Area 51 army base they had just left.

"Hi, guys," said Lily.

"Child," said Jo-Jo, frowning, "what in tarnation are you doin' in my trunk?"

"I wanted to spend a few more days with Ploo," said Lily. "And I always wanted to see Las Vegas."

"I'll bet you didn't tell your mommy or daddy you planned to come with us, did you, darlin'?"

"Of course not," said Lily. "They never would have let me."

"But, sugar, your mom and dad will be all riled up to find you gone. And you can't just skip out on school."

"Oh, Aunt Jo-Jo," said Lily. "It's Friday night and Monday's a holiday. What's the big deal?"

Jo-Jo and the girls got back in the car. Jo-Jo took out her cell phone and dialed Major Paine. "Major, this is Jo-Jo. We're almost all the way back to Vegas and we just found Lily stowed away in the trunk of my car. I'm callin' to tell y'all she's okay."

Lily, Ploo, Lek, and Klatu heard yelling come out of the phone. Jo-Jo held it away from her ear. At last the yelling stopped. Jo-Jo nodded.

"I'll tell her, Major," said Jo-Jo. She flipped the phone shut. "Lily, your dad says you're grounded for a week when you come home."

"Does that mean she will not be allowed to fly?" asked Klatu.

"No, hon, it's an Earth saying. It means

she won't be allowed to leave the house except for school," said Jo-Jo.

Jo-Jo put the car back in gear. Soon they were speeding along the highway again. It was already dark.

Ahead of them in the distance was a tight jumble of twinkling lights. A small, brightly lit city seemed to sprout out of the flat black desert.

"We'll be in Vegas in about ten minutes," Jo-Jo warned. "Y'all better start morphin' into human shape right about now. And you might want to chew up some more of that good English gum." When Klatu, Lek, and Ploo chewed English gum, Earthlings could understand them. At least till the flavor faded.

Ploo handed out the little green gum balls. They began chewing.

"All right, time to morph," said Klatu.

With a soft sound, the three alien children grew upward and outward. Arms and legs grew thicker. Heads grew smaller. Eyes shrank down to the beady little things that Earthlings had.

They'd been on Earth for days now. But all three of them had picked clothes and haircuts from their Earthling Studies textbooks. They still didn't know how old the textbooks were. They had chosen old-fashioned sailor suits. On their feet were button-up shoes. And on their heads sat straw hats with ribbons.

Their new shapes wouldn't last more than an *arp*. One *arp* of Loogl time was close to one hour of Earth time. There were fifty *mynts* in an *arp*. In fifty *mynts*, they'd look like aliens again.

The Elvises Arrive

"Okay, I forgot to tell you, there's been a slight change of plans," said Jo-Jo. "We're movin' to the new rock-and-roll hotel, the Shoobee-Doo-Wah."

"What was wrong with the Titanic?" asked Ploo. The last time they were in Las Vegas, Klatu, Lek, and Ploo had stayed at the Titanic Hotel.

"Well, the floors were so tilted, I was always slidin' to the other side of the room," said Jo-Jo. "I felt like we were goin' to sink any minute. But I got us much cheaper rooms at the Shoobee-Doo-Wah. Besides, it's a really cool place. All the rock stars stay here. See? There it is."

The Cadillac pulled up in the driveway of a strange-looking pink and black hotel. A huge pink electric guitar stuck up out of the ground at the front of the hotel. Its neck was three stories high, and the door was through the sound hole. The giant guitar was outlined in tubes of neon that flashed red, blue, and green.

Jo-Jo got out of the car. Klatu, Lek, Ploo, and Lily followed her. They stared at the front of the Shoobee-Doo-Wah Hotel.

"I am afraid," said Lek.

"Of what?" said Lily.

"Of whatever plays this big guitar," said Lek.

Everybody laughed. Lek was serious.

A small bus drove up the driveway. Six men climbed out of it. They carried silver suitcases and silver guitar cases. They were wearing silver jumpsuits covered with sequins. All the men looked alike. They had wavy black hair and long sideburns. Their upper lips were curled into identical sneers.

"Uh-oh," Klatu whispered. "Look."

"Aliens," whispered Lek.

Jo-Jo chuckled. "Those guys aren't aliens, hon. They're Elvis impersonators. They're probably here for an Elvis convention. There are tons of Elvis conventions in Vegas."

The six men walked through the sound hole of the giant guitar and entered the hotel.

"What is an Elvis percolator?" Lek asked.

"Oh, sorry, darlin'," said Jo-Jo. "That's just somebody who dresses up like Elvis Presley. They try to look and talk and sing exactly like him."

"And who is Pelvis Lesley?" asked Klatu.

"Elvis Presley," said Jo-Jo. "He was one of Earth's most famous rock singers. He performed in Vegas all the time. But he was known and loved all over the world."

They went inside the hotel. The heavy throb of rock-and-roll music filled the lobby like a giant's heartbeat.

The lobby was painted pink and black. The name of the hotel was spelled out in flashing purple neon. On the walls were framed photographs of Elvis, the Beatles, the Rolling Stones, and other famous bands. Between them were framed costumes worn by rock-and-roll stars. Most of the costumes were silver or gold and sparkled in the neon light. Guitars, drumsticks, and microphones that had belonged to famous rockers also hung on the walls. Many of the instruments were flecked with red or gold. They glowed like embers in a fireplace.

Jo-Jo stepped up to the check-in counter to get the keys to their rooms. Klatu, Lek, Ploo, and Lily waited next to her.

One of the Elvises was standing near Klatu. "Hello, Mr. Elvis," said Klatu.

The Elvis looked startled. "What?" he said.

"I said hello," Klatu repeated. "Are you here for a convention?"

The Elvis looked as though he didn't know what to say.

"Can you speak? Or has the *ketzelongo* stolen your tongue?" said Klatu.

"Don't be cruel to a heart that's true," said the Elvis.

"That makes no sense," said Klatu. "Even to me." He shook his head. Earthlings were so weird!

The Elvis looked panicky. He whispered something to the Elvis standing on his other side. Then he hurried away.

"Your friend is not very polite," said Klatu to the second Elvis.

"You ain't nothin' but a hound dog, cryin' all the time," said the second Elvis. "You ain't never caught a rabbit and you ain't no friend of mine." He also walked away from Klatu.

Klatu turned to Lily with a puzzled look on his face.

"Those are all lines from old Elvis Presley songs," Lily explained.

"This proves they are aliens," whispered Lek.

"No it doesn't," said Lily. "It only proves they're weird."

After they checked in, Jo-Jo took the kids up to their new rooms. Like the lobby, the rooms were also pink and black, and pretty fancy. Floor-to-ceiling mirrors covered the walls. Even the ceiling had mirrors.

Lek liked glancing up at the ceiling mirrors to see how he looked to birds—just a round head with shoulders on each side.

The heavy throb of rock-and-roll music was in here, too, but softer.

There were two bedrooms, a sitting room, and a bathroom. The beds were round and far bigger than any Loogling kid needed. The floors were swirly-looking Italian marble. The bathroom had a large guitar-shaped bathtub. The balcony outside had a good view of the main street with all the biggest hotels.

"This is lovely," said Ploo.

"But there are no beds in the third bedroom," said Lek. "I fear someone has stolen them."

"There isn't any third bedroom, hon," said Jo-Jo. "That one is called a sitting room. Do you know what a sitting room is?"

"In the bedrooms, we must lie down," said Klatu. "So in the sitting room, we must only sit."

"Well, something like that," said Jo-Jo.

3

Dangerous Aliens
from Sheboygan

"Okay, kids," said Jo-Jo, "it's way past time we should be asleep. Y'all get washed up for bed."

Lily filled the sink with water. Lek and Klatu stuck their heads into it and blew bubbles. Lily showed Ploo how to use a toothbrush, but Klatu ate the toothpaste before they could use it. When they went to bed, the only one who fell asleep was Jo-Jo.

"I'm too excited to sleep," whispered Lily. "Why don't we explore the hotel?"

"Too dangerous," said Lek. "Earthlings will see that we are aliens. They will throw stones and chase us with burning torches."

"Then we should morph into human shape," said Ploo.

"I don't think you need to do that," said Lily. "It's really late. Everybody in the hotel is probably asleep." Then she thought of something and laughed out loud. "If we meet anybody, we can tell them you're here for an alien convention."

Without morphing, the kids sneaked out for a tour of the hotel. In the basement, they found the Doo-Wop Mall. It had a curved ceiling painted to look like a blue sky with puffy white clouds. The lighting in the sky kept changing. Sometimes it looked the way the sky does in the early morning. Sometimes it looked like afternoon. Sometimes it looked like it does when the sun is just about to set. Sometimes it looked like the dead of night.

The underground mall was laid out like a neighborhood. Stores lined both sides of a cobblestone street. At the street corners stood large gray stone statues of famous rock-and-roll stars. The Beatles. Little Richard. The Rolling Stones. Fats Domino. Chubby Checker. Buddy Holly. Jerry Lee Lewis. Bill Haley and His Comets. Every hour, on the hour, the statues began moving. The first time this happened, Lek jumped about three feet into the air.

"They are alive!" he cried.

"Relax, Lek," said Lily. "They're only moving statues."

This late at night, the stores were closed. Lily and the Looglings looked into the windows of one of the shops. There were CDs of all the great rock-and-roll bands. There were books and photos about rock and roll. There were framed auto-graphed photos. There were guitar-shaped candy dishes and guitar-shaped ashtrays and guitar-shaped guitars. Everything in the shop was rock and roll.

"Klatu, do you know what rock and roll is?" Lily asked.

"Of *course* I know what rock and roll is," said Klatu. "Rock is hard stuff that humans make buildings out of. Roll is round bread that humans eat. It's very tasty with jam or Crazy Glue. The wrap-ping it comes in is tasty, too. I am not a *varna*, you know."

"Okay, just checking," said Lily.

So far, the Doo-Wop Mall had been empty. Now six Elvises turned the corner and came down the cobblestone street.

"Uh-oh," whispered Lek. "It's the aliens."

"Stop being so silly," said Lily. "They're humans, just like me and Jo-Jo." She turned to the nearest Elvis. "Hi," she said. "My friends and I are in town for an alien convention." She winked at Lek and Klatu.

The Elvis looked startled. "What?" he said.

"I said we're in town for an alien convention," said Lily. "How are you doing?"

The Elvis turned to another Elvis.

"How am I doing?" he whispered.

"You are doing fine," whispered the second Elvis.

The first Elvis turned back to Lily.

"I am doing fine," he said.

"Where are you from?" asked Ploo.

The first Elvis looked nervous. He turned to the second Elvis.

"We are from Sheboygan, Wisconsin," said the second Elvis in a too-loud voice. "Wisconsin is a dairy state. It is famed for its delicious milk, its creamery butter, its many fine cheeses, and for the Green Bay Packers football team. Do you know it well?"

"Not that well," said Ploo.

All the Elvises looked relieved.

"When is your convention?" asked Lek.

The Elvises were suddenly nervous again. They huddled together and spoke in whispers. Then the second Elvis turned back to face the kids.

"Of which convention do you speak?" he asked.

"The Elvis convention," said Lek.

"Ah yes, the Elvis convention," said the second Elvis. "Six days. The main landing party will arrive in just six—" He suddenly clapped his hand over his mouth and looked alarmed. The other Elvises glared at him.

"What he meant was, the *convention* will begin in just six days," said a third Elvis.

"I see," said Klatu.

The Elvises whispered together, then hurried away. Halfway down the block, they pulled open a door and went inside. Lily and the Looglings followed them.

The sign on the door was spelled out in flashing purple neon. Ploo read it out loud:

"Between a Rock and a Hard Place Diner," she said. "We never close."

"I am hungry enough to eat many horses," said Klatu. "That is an Earth expression."

"I'm kind of hungry, too," said Lily. "And if we go in there, we can spy on the Elvises."

Klatu went inside. The others followed.

There were lots more mirrors and the same steady rock-and-roll beat as in the lobby.

Klatu, Lek, Ploo, and Lily took seats at the counter. Klatu was much hungrier than the others. Before Lily could stop him, he ate two paper napkins and a large part of his menu.

The waitress came by to take their orders. She wore a waitress uniform with purple sequins.

"Hi," said Lily. "We're in town for an alien convention."

"That's nice," said the waitress. She didn't seem at all surprised to see three aliens with big heads and gray skin sitting at her counter. "What happened to your menu, hon?" she asked Klatu.

"It got . . . torn," said Klatu.

"What happened to the piece that got torn off?" said the waitress.

"I don't know," said Klatu. "Maybe it got . . . eaten."

The waitress blinked twice, and then she went on. "Let me tell you the specials tonight," she said. "First, we have the surf and turf."

"Do you know what surf and turf is, Klatu?" Lily asked.

Klatu nodded. "Of course. Seawater and grass."

"Next we have the ground round," said the waitress.

"The ground round *what*?" said Lek.

"Pardon me?" said the waitress.

"You said you have the ground round," said Lek.

"Right," said the waitress.

"What is the thing you have that is ground and round?" said Lek.

"Oh," said the waitress. "Steak."

"Then why do you not say it is steak?" said Lek. "Why do you make us ask?" He rolled his big black eyes at Klatu. Klatu rolled his big black eyes back at Lek. These Earthlings were too silly!

"I'm sorry," said the waitress. "Now, for dessert, if you folks think you'll want the mud pie or the lava cake, you have to order it before the meal."

"Excuse me," said Ploo. "Do you really

have a pie made out of mud and a cake made out of molten rock?"

"It goes with the seawater and grass," Klatu explained.

"Mud pie is actually chocolate mousse," said the waitress.

"They take a moose and dip it into chocolate," Klatu whispered.

The waitress looked hard at Klatu, Lek, and Ploo. "You folks aren't from around here, are you?" she said.

"They're from back east," said Lily.

"Then that explains it," said the waitress.

With a big sigh, Lily threw her hands in the air. "I'll order for all of us," she said. "We'll have four burgers and four chocolate milk shakes."

"Coming right up," said the waitress. She left.

Klatu spotted the Elvises in a booth at

the back. *Look at the back booth,* Klatu esped.

The Elvises had ordered soup, but no one had told them what to do with it. Four of them sniffed at it and stared. The other two were soaking their hands in it.

I have an idea, Ploo esped to her brothers. *When they leave, let us follow them.*

It is a dangerous idea, esped Lek. *What if they catch us? If they are evil aliens, they may do us great harm. They may torture us! They may pull the flumkins out of our shtoosies!*

I think it is a fine idea! esped Klatu. *I happen to be a great spy. Just watch me. Do everything I do, and they will never notice us.*

Oh brother, esped Ploo.

Big Trouble in the Doo-Wop Mall

"There you are!" said Jo-Jo. She had walked into the diner. "Thank heavens! I've been lookin' everywhere for y'all." Jo-Jo took a seat next to Ploo at the counter.

"I am sorry if we made you worry," said Ploo.

The waitress brought them their food. The kids tasted their burgers.

"Mmm," said Klatu. "I really like these boogers."

"You mean *burgers*," Jo-Jo corrected.

"That is what I said," said Klatu. "They are better than box turtles. You know what would make them even tastier?"

"Ketchup," said Lily.

"It is not necessary for me to catch up," said Klatu. "I am eating as fast as everyone else. But these boogers would taste even better with napkins."

Ploo whispered their plan in Jo-Jo's ear.

As soon as they finished their meal, Klatu, Lek, Ploo, Lily, and Jo-Jo left the restaurant. They waited around the corner. When the Elvises came out, they followed them.

First, the Elvises went into the hotel casino. It looked a lot like the casino in the Titanic Hotel. It had the same swirly brown and green carpet that looked like somebody had thrown up on it. It had the same bright lights and no windows. Like the Titanic Hotel's casino, it had hundreds of slot machines.

Many people stood in front of these machines. They dropped coins into the slots in the machines. Then they pulled the long handles on the sides. Three dials on each machine spun around. The sound of hundreds of coins being dropped into the machines was the same as at the Titanic. The sound of the machines swallowing the coins was the same, too: *Ding-ding-ding-ding. Dong-dong-dong-dong.*

The people at the slot machines didn't even notice that three alien children were standing next to them. They were too interested in what they were doing.

The Elvises didn't seem to know what the slot machines were. Klatu, Lek, and Ploo made fun of them in whispers.

"The Elvises do not understand that these machines are trash cans," Klatu explained to Lily and Jo-Jo. "Those humans have money they no longer want. That's why they put it in these trash cans. They pull the levers to flush the money down."

"Really?" said Jo-Jo. "I don't think that's the way it works."

"Oh yes," said Klatu. "Trust me, Jo-Jo. I read all about this in Earthling Studies. Sometimes the trash cans get clogged and the money comes back out. Then the poor human has to put all the coins back into the trash can until they are gone again."

"I see," said Jo-Jo. She looked at Lily and shrugged.

Next the Elvises went to the roulette wheel.

"Roulette is something we Looglings do very well," Lek told Lily proudly. "At the

Titanic casino, we won so much money that we couldn't get rid of it. They made us carry it with us when we left. It was very heavy. We still have two bags of it in Jo-Jo's trunk."

"So that's what those things were," said Lily. "They kept falling over on me when I was in there."

Finally, the Elvises got ready to leave the casino. Klatu, Lek, Ploo, Lily, and Jo-Jo followed them back downstairs to the Doo-Wop Mall. There the Elvises seemed to vanish.

"Where did they go?" Lek whispered.

Klatu, Lek, and Ploo looked all around. The mall was eerie and empty of tourists. Ploo could barely make out the statues of the rock stars. Lek was right—it was spooky to see them moving in the nearly dark mall.

As Jo-Jo and Lily passed by, the statues

of the Beatles suddenly came to life. Paul and George grabbed Lily and Jo-Jo. Ringo tore off his mop-top wig. Under it was a black pompadour and sideburns. It was the evil Elvises!

Lily screamed. Jo-Jo punched out at them. It didn't work. Even when Klatu, Lek, and Ploo tried to help, it was hopeless. There were just too few Looglings and too many Elvises.

Lily and Jo-Jo were dragged off into the dark.

5

The Secret Hideout of the Evil Elvises

"Where are you dragging us?" asked Lily.

"That is for me to know and for you to find out," said one of the Elvises who were dragging Lily. "I will give you some advice, though. It will not help you to straggle."

"Straggle?" said Lily. "Don't you mean it won't help to *struggle*? *Straggle* means 'to lag behind.'"

"Do you mock the way I speak?" asked the Elvis. He seemed angry.

"No, I'm just trying to help you speak better," said Lily.

"I think I speak your language good, coming where I come from."

"Where *do* you come from?" Lily asked.

"I cannot tell you that," said the Elvis.

"Why not?" said Lily.

"Because," said the Elvis, "you are an Earthling."

"What would you tell me if I wasn't an Earthling?" Lily asked.

"That we come from planet Graceland."

"Silence!" yelled another Elvis. "There is no talking to prisoners!"

"I know that!" yelled the Elvis who was dragging Lily. "Do you not think I know that?"

The four Elvises who were dragging Lily and Jo-Jo stopped before a life-sized statue of Elvis Presley playing the guitar.

The Elvis closest to the statue turned a key on the neck of the guitar. With a groaning sound, the entire statue slid slowly to the left, revealing a hidden doorway.

The four Elvises who were dragging Lily and Jo-Jo opened the door and went through it.

Inside, the room was dark. It smelled musty, like an attic where somebody's grandma stored her old furniture and photo albums. The only lights that Lily could see came from the glowing red, purple, and blue dials on banks of electronic equipment. Two more Elvises sat in front of the dials.

"Who are you people?" Jo-Jo demanded.

"None of your business," said one of the Elvises.

"What are y'all plannin' to do with us?" Jo-Jo demanded.

"Also none of your business," said the
Elvis. "Plus which, we do not speak to prisoners. That is our law."

"Well, you're already speakin' to prisoners," said Jo-Jo. "So y'all have broken your own law."

The Elvises all looked at one another. "She makes a good point," one admitted.

Klatu, Lek, and Ploo were searching for Lily and Jo-Jo. But they'd had no luck. Their failure made them feel more tired than ever.

"They are gone," said Klatu.

"How can they have vanished without a trace?" said Ploo.

"Perhaps they were teleported to another world," said Lek.

Sadly, they returned to their rooms. Although it was still beautiful, Ploo couldn't stand seeing her unhappy face in the mirrors. She stuck her tongue out at her reflection.

"Poor Lily and Jo-Jo," said Lek. "We shall never see them again. Now Jo-Jo can never drive us to meet the spaceship the Great Ones are sending back for us."

"And if they do not send it, she can never build us a new one from scratching," said Klatu.

"We are doomed," said Lek. "We shall never see our beloved planet Loogl again. We are stuck forever on a weird planet where they eat seawater, grass, mud, and molten rock."

Ploo did not say anything. She had begun trying to find Lily and Jo-Jo. Ploo was very good with her mind. She could do things Lek and Klatu couldn't. She cast out a thought net that was like a huge fishing net. She was trying to snag any stray ideas that might have floated out of Lily's mind. Now she pulled in the net and looked at all the thoughts flopping around in it.

Nothing seemed like it came from Lily.

Ploo formed a picture of Lily in her mind. Then she tried to tune in to her thoughts like tuning in stations on a radio. At first, there was nothing but static. Then Ploo thought she heard little parts of sentences: *". . . and they're also stupid and . . ."* *". . . so why don't they just let us go . . ."*

Was that Lily? It sounded like her voice, but Ploo couldn't tell for sure. She adjusted her tuning. *". . . and for sure, my daddy would kick their butts all the way back to planet Graceland!"*

Yes! That was Lily! No doubt about it now!

Ploo tried to zero in on where these thoughts were coming from. It was definitely in the Shoobee-Doo-Wah Hotel. It was definitely in the Doo-Wop Mall. Ploo tuned in to a mind map of the hotel's mall. The map showed the walls, the electrical system, and the pipes. It showed the air-conditioning ducts that carried cool air to all the rooms. A red light seemed to flash where the air-conditioning ducts met in a basement storage room. That must be where Lily was!

How could Ploo and her brothers rescue Lily and Jo-Jo? If they just went up to the storage room door and knocked, they'd get caught. They could crawl through the air-conditioning ducts. But Looglings weren't good at crawling. It hurt their knees.

Maybe they could morph into something smaller than Looglings and slip right through the ducts. What if they morphed into something the size of a *ketzelongo*— what Earthlings called a cat?

6

Cat Commandos to the Rescue

I have never had a tail before, **Lek esped**. What are you supposed to do with it when you sit down? Are you supposed to sit on it or what? And these whiskers are tickling me like crazy. Are they supposed to be this tickly?

None of us have had tails or whiskers before, either, Lek, **Ploo esped**. Stop complaining and let us get through this air-conditioning duct. I think we turn left at the next corner.

Lek, Ploo, and Klatu, now in cat bodies,

crept through the ducts in the walls of the Doo-Wop Mall. Their tails swished back and forth. Their ears turned backward and forward. They were trying to get used to all the new sounds they could hear. Tiny flutterings, tiny squeaks.

When they got to the corner of the duct, a small, furry face peeked out at them. A mouse!

The mouse took one look at the three cats coming toward him and ran off in the opposite direction. In a flash, Klatu was racing after him.

Klatu! esped Ploo. *Forget that mouse and get back here!*

But it looks so delicious! esped Klatu.

How do you know what it will taste like? Ploo esped. *You are a Loogling, not a ketzelongo.*

If you eat that mouse, you will probably get sick to your stomach. You will have terrible gas pains, esped Lek. *Now come back here and help us rescue Lily and Jo-Jo.*

Oh, all right, esped Klatu. He crept back to his sister and brother, whiskers drooping, his tail between his legs.

After five more minutes, Lek, Ploo, and Klatu found where the air-conditioning duct blew cool air into the storage room. They peeked through the grate. Both

Looglings and *ketzelongos* can see well in the dark, but there was not much to see in the storage room. They saw some red, blue, and purple lights, the kind they had on their spaceship. They didn't see either Lily or Jo-Jo.

Ploo pressed her nose up against the grate. She meowed as loudly as she could.

Inside the room, they heard somebody get up. Ploo meowed again. Somebody came up to the grate. A little girl. Lily.

Ploo meowed again.

"Oh, look, Aunt Jo-Jo," said Lily. "It's a kitty."

"A kitty?" said Jo-Jo's voice. "How could a kitty get into an air-conditionin' duct, darlin'?"

"Come here and see," said Lily.

Jo-Jo came to see. There didn't seem to be any Elvises in the storage room. Had they gone back to their hotel rooms to sleep? Klatu and Lek pressed their noses against the grate, too.

Lily, it is us—Klatu, Lek, and Ploo, Ploo esped. She tried to get through to Lily's mind. But her cat brain felt very different from her Loogling brain. We have come to rescue you! she added.

"It's *three* kitties, Aunt Jo-Jo!" said Lily. "How'd three kitties ever get into that vent?"

"I sure don't hardly know, sugar," said Jo-Jo.

Lily, can you hear me? Ploo esped. You must open the grate and climb into the duct. Quickly, before the Elvises come back!

"Do you think the kitties are hungry, Aunt Jo-Jo?" said Lily.

It is hopeless, Lek esped. They cannot hear us. Maybe it is because we are now ketzelongos. They are doomed.

51

"I wouldn't be at all surprised if they were hungry, hon," said Jo-Jo. "We don't know how long they've been stuck there."

Meow at them, Ploo esped to her brothers. *We must somehow get through to them.*

Klatu, Lek, and Ploo meowed their little hearts out.

"They *are* hungry, Aunt Jo-Jo," said Lily. "Can't you do anything?"

"Well, child," said Jo-Jo, "we sure don't have any food. But I guess I could open the grate and let 'em out."

Jo-Jo took a key chain out of her pocket. Attached to it was a small screwdriver. She used it to unscrew the four screws that held the grate in place.

"There," she said. "Come on out, kitties."

Klatu, Lek, and Ploo didn't move. They just continued to meow.

Jo-Jo reached into the duct to get them.

Klatu, Lek, and Ploo backed away from her. Then they came forward again and meowed some more.

"Those pussycats seem to be afraid of me," said Jo-Jo.

"No, I think they want us to follow them," said Lily.

"I don't know," said Jo-Jo. "It looks kinda small for me. But we can give it a try. You first, darlin'."

Jo-Jo grabbed Lily and lifted her into the opening. Lily scampered into the duct. Jo-Jo got a leg up. She was just about to try and squeeze through when the door of the storage room opened.

It was the Elvises!

"The Earthlings are escaping!" yelled an Elvis. "Stop them!"

The evil Elvises rushed forward and grabbed Jo-Jo by the legs.

"Crawl, Lily!" yelled Jo-Jo. "Crawl for your life!"

Running for Your Life on Paws

Lily crawled as fast as she could. She crawled like six evil Elvises were after her. Which they were. She couldn't see well in the dark ducts, but she tried to keep up with the cats. When she fell behind, they waited for her.

At last, they reached the small trapdoor where they'd entered the air-conditioning duct. Klatu stuck his head out and looked around.

All clear, Klatu esped. He hopped through the opening to the ground.

Suddenly fierce barking began.

Okay, maybe <u>not</u> all clear, Klatu esped. He jumped right back into the duct.

Below them were two gigantic German shepherds. They were barking and growling and making tremendous leaps into the air.

They will tear us to pieces! Lek esped. *What chance do three <u>ketzelongos</u> and a human girl have against two huge guard dogs?*

Not much chance at all, esped Ploo. *But what if we weren't <u>ketzelongos</u>? What if we were . . . leopards?*

Leopards? But we just morphed into <u>ketze-longos</u>. Can we morph again so soon without horribly hurting ourselves? Lek esped.

Maybe, maybe not, Ploo esped. *A leopard is just a big <u>ketzelongo</u>. Let me try it first. If it works, you do it, too.*

Below her, the guard dogs snapped and growled and prowled. Ploo brought a picture of a leopard into her mind. She counted to three and began to stretch. Her tail grew longer. Her whiskers grew longer. Her paws grew bigger. Her small cat teeth grew into long leopard fangs. Her claws curved into long, sharp points.

In the dim light coming through the trapdoor, Lily saw what was happening. She gasped.

"What . . . ? I can't believe . . . Ploo, is that you?" she asked.

In mid-morph, the half-leopard, half-cat turned toward the little girl. She touched her very gently with her large paw. She was careful to keep her sharp claws inside their pads. Then she gave the girl a lick with her long, scratchy tongue.

"Oh, Ploo!" said Lily. The little girl

threw her arms around the leopard and gave her a big hug. "I should have known it was you!"

I love you, Lily, Ploo esped, knowing Lily couldn't hear her. We will keep you safe from guard dogs and evil Elvises.

Ploo continued morphing. Her legs grew long and powerful. Her backbone lengthened. Her stomach filled out. Her golden coat became dappled with black splotches. One more growth spurt to her powerful tail and the morphing was complete.

Ploo stuck her head through the trapdoor. Her ears flattened against her head. Her lips drew back, revealing long white fangs. She let loose a high-pitched screech that scared not only the dogs but her brothers. Ploo hopped to the ground, growling.

Yelping with fright, the guard dogs galloped away into the mall.

People in Las Vegas are no longer surprised by anything they see. So no one in the Shoobee-Doo-Wah Hotel was shocked when two guard dogs dashed past. And no one batted an eye when a little blond girl, two cats, and a leopard paraded by and got into an elevator.

Back in their suite, Klatu, Lek, and Ploo collapsed onto the floor. Within seconds, they fell asleep. Morphing from one shape to another was very, very tiring.

An hour later, they woke up.

"Did you find out anything about the Elvises?" Ploo asked Lily.

"They're mean and stupid," said Lily. "You were right about them, Lek. They are aliens from a planet called Graceland. They know everything about Elvis Presley. They have learned to be as much like him as possible. They even named their planet after his home. And the aliens are scouts for a big invasion. In just five days, a huge attack force will be landing here. They call it a 'grace-landing.'"

"Then we have two jobs," said Ploo.

"Getting out of town, and making sure

they do not know where we went?" said Klatu.

"No, rescuing Jo-Jo, and warning the people of Las Vegas," said Ploo.

"So getting out of town is our *third* job," said Klatu.

"We are not getting out of town, Klatu," said Ploo. "We are staying here to help fight the evil Elvises."

"What makes you think humans will believe they're about to be attacked by creatures from another planet who look like Elvis Presley?" said Klatu.

"When we tell them all the facts, they will believe us," said Lek.

8

The Elvises Are Coming! The Elvises Are Coming!

The four children were ushered into the office of the manager of the Shoobee-Doo-Wah Hotel. Several video screens hung from the ceiling. They weren't tuned to TV shows. They all showed different places in the hotel. Most of the places were in the casino.

The manager, whose name was Mr. Bosco, was chewing on a cigar the size of a cucumber. He was completely bald, but he wore something odd on top of his head. Klatu was puzzled. It was shiny and black and supposed to be hair. But it looked more like a coaster on which to put a cold drink.

"Good morning, kids. Good morning," said Mr. Bosco. "What can the Shoobee-Doo-Wah Hotel do for you on such a fine day?"

"We came to warn you," said Ploo.

"Warn me?" said Mr. Bosco with a smile. "What did you come to warn me about?"

"In five days, we are going to be invaded by hundreds of Elvises," said Klatu.

"*Thousands* of Elvises," said Lek.

Mr. Bosco chuckled.

"I know all about that," he said.

"You do?" said Klatu.

"Of course," said Mr. Bosco. "It happens every year. Several times a year, in fact. Hordes of Elvis impersonators come

to Vegas for their conventions. It brings us a lot of business. We're always delighted to see them."

"You do not understand," said Lek. "These are not normal Elvises. These are aliens from planet Graceland. They are coming to take over Las Vegas! They will

take prisoners! And maybe they will even kill Earthlings—er, people."

Mr. Bosco laughed uproariously at this.

"You kids have a marvelous imagination," he said. "Marvelous. That's not such a bad little idea to amuse the tourists, by the way. Have a bunch of Elvis impersonators pretend to be aliens from outer space. Pretend to take over the town. I'll suggest it to the mayor. Maybe we'll do it next year. Have a big parade and fireworks. If we do it, you kids can be our guests of honor. Well, thanks for stopping by."

Mr. Bosco stood up. It was the signal for them to leave.

"Mr. Bosco, we didn't make this up," said Lily. "It's real. It's happening here in five days. It won't be fun. It will be a disaster."

"Okay, honey," said Mr. Bosco, chuckling again. "Thanks for telling me."

He opened his office door and ushered them out.

"All right," said Klatu when they were out in the hallway. "I thought that went pretty well."

"You thought it went well?" said Ploo.

"Sure," said Klatu. "He might make us

guests of honor next year. What *is* a guest of honor, anyway?"

When they went to the Las Vegas police, they were treated politely. They were asked to wait on a worn wooden bench. Lots of people must have had to wait on that bench over the years, because they'd carved their initials into it.

If Klatu, Lek, and Ploo had known, they wouldn't have morphed into human shape till they were just about to enter the police station. They kept nervously looking at the *arp*-timers on their wrists.

Their human shapes would begin to melt in less than an *arp*. They had less than twenty *mynts* to go.

Finally, they were called into the detective's office. By then, even their English gum was losing its flavor.

"Well, now, what can I do for you kids?" said Detective Ambrose. He had a blond buzz cut and a very sunburned face.

"We come to . . . warning you about the Elvises," said Klatu. As his gum's flavor faded, he was losing his ability to speak. Even worse, he could feel his head growing larger.

The detective smiled. "Those Elvises aren't giving you any trouble, I hope," he said.

"These not . . . *normal* Elvises," said Ploo. The middle of her head was starting to itch. She knew her antenna might pop out any second now.

"Yeah, sometimes they don't act too normal," said Detective Ambrose.

"Is . . . *invasion* of Elvises coming," said Lek. "In five days. We doomed." He saw that the skin on his hand was turning very gray. He put it behind his back.

"I know what you mean," said the detective, chuckling. "When they come to town for those conventions, it does feel like an invasion."

"No, no," said Ploo. "Is *real* invasion. Is . . . invasion of alien beings . . . from other planet."

"It sure seems like that," said the detective, still chuckling. "Say, where are you kids from? Russia? Poland? You don't sound like you're from around here."

"Please, sir," said Lily. "You have to listen to us. We have to warn everyone. A landing party of aliens from another planet is going to attack in just five days. They look like Elvises, but they're evil aliens. And they're very dangerous. We're not making this up."

The detective looked at them for several seconds. The smile on his sunburned face dissolved like a lump of sugar in a cup of hot chocolate. He suddenly seemed tired.

"Okay, kids," said Detective Ambrose. "Fun's over. I gotta get back to work. Are your parents outside?"

"No," said Klatu. He held both his arms up to hide his rapidly growing head.

"Yes," said Ploo. She clapped her hand over her head just as her antenna squirted out.

"Parents on planet Loogl," said Lek. He tried to pull his growing head down into his shirt like a turtle into its shell.

Klatu, Lek, and Ploo raced out of the detective's office. Lily turned to go.

"They aren't feeling well," she said. "Spoiled cheeseburgers, I think."

9

A Visit with Billy-Bob Underpense

Back at the hotel room, the kids were feeling discouraged. The mayor was no help. The police were no help. They were on their own.

"It's up to us to rescue Jo-Jo and save Las Vegas from the evil Elvises," said Ploo. "Any ideas how to do that?"

Everybody started thinking hard.

Klatu jumped up.

"I know! I know!" he said. "We could

get a lot of paint and brushes and we could disguise Las Vegas. From the air, we could make it look like there are no buildings or people here, only sand. They would think they were in the wrong place and go away."

"So we'd have to paint every building in the whole city?" said Lily.

"Well, yes, of course," said Klatu.

"Thank you, Klatu," said Ploo. "Any more ideas?"

Klatu sat down. Then he jumped up again.

"I have an even better idea!" he said. "We could make everybody in Las Vegas look like Elvis. The aliens would be so confused, they would go crazy and leave."

"So we'd have to get at least a million Elvis wigs and jumpsuits?" said Ploo.

"Oh, probably a lot more than that," said Klatu.

"Thank you, Klatu," said Ploo. "Any more ideas?"

Everybody was quiet. They were thinking. Even Klatu was thinking.

"The alien Elvises are trained to be just like the real Elvis, right?" said Lek.

"Yes," said Lily.

"Maybe we need to know more about the real Elvis," said Lek. "Then we can figure out a way to stop them."

"Who could tell us more about the real Elvis?" said Klatu.

"What about a real Elvis impersonator?" said Lily.

Lily got the Yellow Pages phone book out of a drawer and looked up *Elvis Impersonators*. One was listed at an address about three blocks from their hotel.

Klatu, Lek, and Ploo morphed into their human forms, and the four kids set out. They soon found the house and knocked on the door. It was made of pink stucco, and there were plastic palm trees in the front yard.

The door was opened by someone who looked a lot like Elvis Presley.

"Come in," he said. "I am Elvis. Well, actually, my name is Billy-Bob Underpense. Y'all can call me either Elvis or Billy-Bob."

Billy-Bob Underpense had wavy black hair and long sideburns. His upper lip curled into a sneer. He wore a jumpsuit covered with gold sequins. He looked pretty much like the fake Elvises. The only difference was that Billy-Bob didn't try to take them prisoner.

"I am Ploo," said Ploo. "And this is Lek, Klatu, and Lily."

Billy-Bob's house was crazy-looking. There were potted plastic palm trees inside,

too. The walls had been painted with scenes of swimming, surfing, and colorful sunsets. Straw mats covered the floors. The furniture was made of wicker. From somewhere came the slippery, slidey sound of Hawaiian guitars. Elvis Presley had loved Hawaii.

"Tell us about Elvis," said Lily.

"What would y'all like to know about him?" asked Billy-Bob.

"Tell us what he loved," said Ploo.

"Tell us what he hated," said Klatu.

"Tell us what he was afraid of," said Lek.

"Tell us his favorite foods," said Lily.

Billy-Bob leaned back in his wicker chair. He thoughtfully stroked his sideburns.

"Elvis was afraid of the ocean and large crowds," he said. "He hated fish and bullies. His favorite food was peanut-butter-and-mashed-banana sandwiches."

The kids looked at each other and smiled.

"I know what we can do!" said Klatu.

"So do I," said Lek.

"Me too," said Lily.

"I think we have what we need now, Billy-Bob," said Ploo. "Thank you very much."

The Elvis Invasion

Klatu, Lek, Ploo, and Lily went back to their rooms at the Shoobee-Doo-Wah Hotel. Between them, they came up with a plan. It was a pretty good plan.

"You know something?" said Lily. "This might really work."

"It *better* work," said Ploo.

"If not, Earth is doomed!" said Lek.

The three Looglings and one little Earthling girl left the hotel. They grabbed the two bags of money out of Jo-Jo's pink

Cadillac. Each went to buy the things they needed.

Lily bought rolls and rolls of electrical wiring. Ploo bought sound-effects recordings of crashing waves and roaring crowds. Together they bought a sound system with many gigantic speakers. They set up speakers in an area at the edge of the Vegas Strip.

Lek bought loaves and loaves of white bread. Klatu bought gallons and gallons of peanut butter. They bought bunches and bunches of overripe bananas. Together they made a huge number of sandwiches. Then Klatu ate ten of them. "Elvis had good taste in food," he said.

They looked out the window at the black Las Vegas sky. In the east, it was beginning to turn lighter. Only an hour or two was left for sleep.

The evil Elvises would invade sometime tomorrow.

Klatu, Lek, Ploo, and Lily were as ready as they'd ever be.

At exactly 9 a.m. the next day, the invasion began. A gigantic mother ship floated soundlessly overhead. It was silver and round and looked like the Goodyear Blimp, only about twenty times bigger. A gentle shower of little pink somethings drifted to Earth from the mother ship.

"Look," said Lek, pointing.

Klatu, Lek, Ploo, and Lily were already outside. They had laid out all the sandwiches. They had checked out all the speakers.

Klatu rubbed his big black eyes. *Those pink somethings look familiar,* he esped.

Yes, esped Lek. *I know them, too. They are . . .*

Pink Cadillacs! Ploo finished for him.

The pink Cadillacs had sharky fins, just like Jo-Jo's. Just like the real Elvis's. There

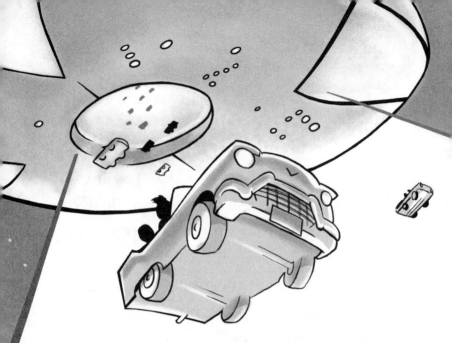

were hundreds of them. They kept on drifting out of the mother ship. They looked like big pink snowflakes with fins.

The tourists were delighted. They thought it was another fabulous Vegas show. They poured out of the hotels and casinos to watch.

"Look!" one shouted. "Pink Cadillacs! What will they think of next?"

"This is even better than the volcanoes!" shouted another.

"Thank heavens I've got my camera!" shouted a third. "I can't wait to show the folks at home!"

The pink Cadillacs began touching down on the ground. When they landed, the doors opened wide.

Out of the pink Cadillacs climbed Elvises in silver sequined jumpsuits. All the Elvises held pink electric guitars. One of the Elvises pointed the end of his guitar at a station wagon parked by the side of the road. A red beam shot out of the guitar and hit the station wagon. It exploded into a million pieces.

All the tourists cheered. All but the owner of the station wagon.

"Those are dangerous guitars," said Klatu.

"They are not guitars. They are ray guns," said Ploo.

"I knew that," said Klatu. "Do you not think I knew that?"

The Elvises began to sing and play, "You ain't nothin' but a hound dog." The way the song was played numbed human brains and hurt human eardrums.

The tourists began to scream. Lily clapped her hands over her ears, but the sound didn't seem to bother Klatu, Lek, or Ploo. Then, strangely, the Elvises stopped playing. Nose after Elvis nose sniffed the air.

The Elvises smelled the sandwiches. The hundreds of sandwiches the kids had made. The smell was overwhelming. And the Elvises couldn't resist it.

"Ooooh! Peanut butter and mashed banana!" they cried. "Yummy!"

Following the smell of hundreds of

peanut-butter-and-mashed-banana sandwiches, the Elvises ran into the corner of
the lot. They didn't notice the speakers
the kids had placed there. Hundreds of
Elvises grabbed for sandwiches.

"Now?" said Klatu.

"Now?" said Lek.

"Now!" said Ploo.

Klatu turned on the sound system. He
turned on the sound-effects recordings of
ocean surf. He turned on the sound-effects
recordings of rioting crowds. He blasted
the Elvises with painfully loud bursts of
sound.

The Elvises were terrified. They began
to scream.

"No!" they shouted. "We hate crowds!"

"Help!" they shouted. "We hate the
ocean!" They began to shake uncontrollably.

"Bless my soul, what's a-wrong with

me?" they sang. "I'm shakin' like a man on a fuzzy tree!"

Their sideburns quivered. Their wavy black hairdos shivered.

Silver sequins dropped from their jumpsuits and plinked on the ground.

And then something even weirder began to happen. The evil Elvises' skin began to melt like wax from a candle. It dripped down their faces like chocolate syrup. It ran down their arms and legs like warm ice cream.

The tourists who hadn't run away stared with open mouths. The Elvises' skin dissolved. And the tourists could see what was underneath—the aliens' true shapes. The tourists gasped. The aliens had large, smooth heads. And big black eyes. And long, slimy tentacles studded with round suction cups.

"Yuck!" cried Lily. "They look like giant octopuses, only creepier! I feel like barfing!"

"I do not know what *barfing* means," said Klatu. "But I prefer that you do not do it on me."

The aliens dropped their guitar-shaped ray guns and crawled toward their Cadillacs as fast as their long pink tentacles let them go. They slithered into their cars. The doors snapped shut behind them.

The Cadillacs began to rise slowly off the ground. They rose higher and higher. The higher they rose, the tinier they looked. Then a panel opened in the belly of the mother ship. All the pink cars were sucked inside. The panel slid shut. The mother ship shot upward and vanished without a sound.

"It worked!" yelled Klatu.

"I never thought it would work!" Lek shouted.

"I knew it would work!" yelled Ploo.

"We saved Las Vegas from the evil Elvises!" shouted Lily.

"Now we have only one more job to do," said Ploo.

"Eat breakfast?" said Klatu.

"No, rescue Jo-Jo, you *varna*!" said Ploo.

She, Klatu, Lek, and Lily raced to the Shoobee-Doo-Wah Hotel and ran downstairs to the Doo-Wop Mall in the basement.

At first, they couldn't open the door of the storage room. Ploo tried by using her mind. They heard clicking noises inside the lock, but it didn't open. Finally, Klatu bit through the lock.

The kids cheered.

But when they opened the door, Jo-Jo wasn't there.

"Jo-Jo!" cried Lily. "We've come to rescue you! Where are you? Are you okay?"

There was only silence. Then they heard the sound of footsteps in the dark. Jo-Jo staggered out, blinking in the bright light. She looked tired and hungry but happy to see them.

"Thank you! Thank you!" said Jo-Jo, hugging everybody. "Y'all are my heroes. Hey, what was all that racket I heard out there?"

"Oh, nothing much," said Ploo with a smile.

"Just an invasion of evil Elvises from planet Graceland," said Lily.

"Elvises carrying deadly ray-gun guitars," Lek added.

"Nothing we could not handle," Klatu said. He gave a casual shrug. "Trust me, Jo-Jo. There is no Elvis percolator in the universe who is a match for Looglings!"

Klatu, Lek, and Ploo are headed to Hollywood!
Don't miss the fifth exciting book in
the weird planet series.

by Dan Greenburg
illustrated by Macky Pamintuan